This book belongs to

_____

_____

Ladybird

A catalogue record for this book is available from the British Library

Published by Ladybird Books Ltd
27 Wrights Lane London W8 5TZ
A Penguin Company
© LADYBIRD BOOKS LTD MCMXCIX
LADYBIRD and the device of a Ladybird are trademarks of Ladybird Books Ltd

Rapunzel

a traditional tale
retold by Ronne Randall

illustrated by Jan Lewis

Long, long ago
there lived a man and woman who wanted a child more than anything else in the world.

At last, after many years, they were thrilled to learn that they would soon have a baby. One evening, the woman stood at her window, looking down at the garden next door. It was full of delicious vegetables.

No one she knew had ever been into the garden, for it was surrounded by a high, forbidding wall.

"Those fresh green rampion leaves look so tempting," the woman sighed.
"I think I will die if I can't eat some in a salad." And she begged her husband to get some for her.

At first the man refused, for he had heard that the garden belonged to a witch. But his wife grew so ill with longing for the rampion, that he climbed the wall and gathered some for her.

He was just about to leave when he suddenly found himself face to face with the witch.

"How dare you steal from my garden?" she shrieked.

"Please have mercy," the man begged. "This rampion is for my wife, who is expecting a baby. She is very ill."

"Very well," said the witch. "Take as much as you like, but on one condition. You must give your child to me as soon as it is born."

Terrified, the man agreed, then fled.

From then on, the man went to the witch's garden every day to gather rampion for his wife. She soon grew strong and healthy again.

A few months later, the couple's baby was born – a beautiful, rosy-cheeked little girl. But when the baby was just two hours old, the witch arrived.

"Remember your promise," she said to the man. "The baby belongs to me!" And she carried the little girl away.

The witch took the baby to a faraway cottage. She named the girl Rapunzel, the word in the witch's language for the rampion that grew in the walled garden.

The witch looked after Rapunzel well,
and gave her everything she needed.
But the little girl was never
allowed to stray further than
the cottage garden, and she
never saw anyone but the witch.

As time passed, Rapunzel grew into a
beautiful little girl with long, golden hair.

When Rapunzel was twelve years old, the witch took her deep into the forest, and she locked her in a high stone tower.

The tower had neither door nor stairs. There was just one small window through which Rapunzel could look out at the world.

Every day, the witch came and stood below the window, calling,

"Rapunzel, Rapunzel, let down your hair for me."

Then Rapunzel would let her long, golden hair out of the window, so it tumbled down the high wall. This was the witch's special ladder to the top of Rapunzel's tower.

To help to pass away the long, lonely hours, Rapunzel gazed out of her tiny window and sang with the birds. And so the years went by.

One day the king's son was riding through the forest, and he heard Rapunzel singing. Enchanted by her beautiful voice, he followed the sound to the tower. But he could find no way to get inside. So he hid among the trees and waited to see if anyone would come.

Sure enough, the witch soon arrived.
When the prince saw how she got
into the tower, he decided to try it too.

That evening, after the witch had gone, the prince stood below Rapunzel's window and called,

"Rapunzel, Rapunzel, let down your hair for me."

A moment later, Rapunzel's golden hair
came tumbling from the tower window
and up climbed the prince.

Rapunzel was shocked to see the prince
coming in through her window. She had
never seen anyone but the witch.

But the prince spoke kindly and gently to
Rapunzel, and soon she lost her fear.

After that, the prince came to see Rapunzel every evening. The pair quickly fell in love, and the prince asked Rapunzel to be his wife. But they couldn't get married while Rapunzel was still in the tower.

"Bring me a skein of silk each time you come," Rapunzel told the prince. "I will weave the silk into a ladder. As soon as it's long enough, I will climb down from the tower and we can run away together."

The prince did as Rapunzel asked, and in just a few weeks the ladder was nearly ready. Only a little more silk was needed.

All this time, the witch suspected nothing.
Then one day, as she was climbing in
through the window, the young girl
absent-mindedly asked the witch,
"Why is it that you feel so much heavier
than the prince?"

The witch flew into a rage. "Ungrateful
wretch!" she screamed. "I have tried to
protect you from the world, and you have
deceived me!" Seizing a pair of scissors, she
cut off Rapunzel's long, golden hair –

snippety-snap!

Then she took Rapunzel away from the
tower to a faraway desert, and left her
there to wander all alone.

That night the witch tied the golden plait to the window, and then she waited in the tower. At last she heard the prince call,

"Rapunzel, Rapunzel, let down your hair."

The golden hair came tumbling down the tower wall, and the prince climbed straight up.

He was horrified to see the
witch instead of Rapunzel.

"The bird has flown the nest,"
the witch cackled. "You will
never see your beloved
Rapunzel again!"

Filled with grief and despair, the prince turned and leapt from the tower window.

He fell down into a thicket of brambles, which scratched his eyes and blinded him. Grief-stricken and sightless, he stumbled through the forest.

The prince wandered in this way for months, living on wild berries and rain water. His clothes were in tatters and his hair was matted, but he neither knew nor cared.

After a long time, he came to a desert. As he staggered among the rocks, a beautiful sound reached him. It was the sweet voice of Rapunzel, singing in the distance.

Now filled with
hope and joy, the
prince hurried
towards the voice.

Rapunzel recognised the prince at once, despite his ragged appearance. She hugged him and wept with happiness.

Two of Rapunzel's tears fell on the prince's blind eyes. All at once, his eyes were healed and his sight came back – and the first thing he saw was Rapunzel's smiling face.

Vowing never to be parted from her again, the prince took Rapunzel in his arms and carried her back to his kingdom.

THERE THE TWO WERE MARRIED,
AND LIVED A LONG AND
HAPPY LIFE TOGETHER.

About the illustrator

JAN LEWIS is a popular children's book
illustrator and has worked for a number
of international publishers.
She studied art and design at the
Bath Academy of Art and primary teaching
in Exeter. She lives with her husband
and two sons in Oxfordshire.
They have a dog, three cats, a parrot,
several chickens and some ducks.